DINOSAURS
BEFORE DARK

MARY POPE OSBORNE'S
MAGIC TREE HOUSE

DINOSAURS BEFORE DARK

illustrated by
Antonio Javier Caparo

A STEPPING STONE BOOK™
Random House 🏠 New York

Visit us on the Web!
rhcbooks.com
MagicTreeHouse.com

Educators and librarians, for a variety of teaching tools, visit us at
RHTeachersLibrarians.com

Library of Congress Cataloging-in-Publication Data is available upon request.
ISBN 978-0-593-12726-1 (special edition hardcover)
ISBN 978-0-593-12727-8 (special edition lib. bdg.)

The artist used a mix of digital and traditional tools, but mostly digital (Adobe Photoshop),
to create the illustrations for this book.
The text of this book is set in 14-point Century Expanded Medium.
Interior design by Sarah Hokanson

MANUFACTURED IN CHINA
10 9 8 7 6 5 4 3 2 1   First Deluxe Edition 2020

This book has been officially leveled by using the F&P Text Level Gradient™ Leveling System.

For Linda and Mallory,
who took the trip with me.

Contents

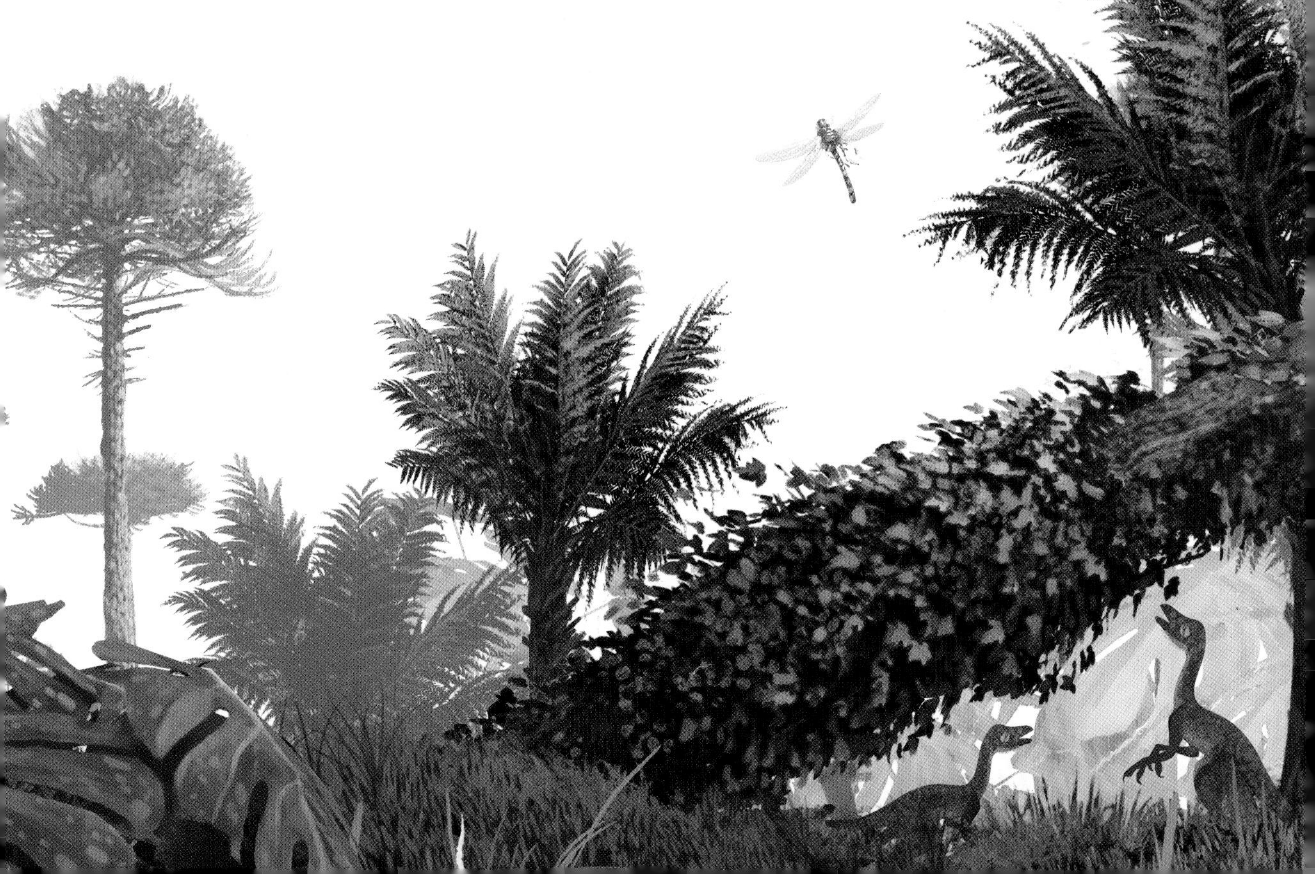

CHAPTER ONE

INTO THE WOODS

"Help! A monster!" said Annie.

"Yeah, sure," said Jack. "A real monster in Frog Creek, Pennsylvania."

"Run, Jack!" said Annie. She ran up the road.

Oh, brother, thought Jack. This is what he got for spending time with his seven-year-old sister.

Annie loved pretend stuff. But Jack was eight and a half. He liked *real* things.

"Watch out, Jack! The monster's coming!" said Annie.

Jack didn't say anything.

"Come on, Jack, I'll race you!" said Annie.

"No, thanks," said Jack.

Annie raced alone into the woods.

Jack looked at the sky. The sun was about to set.

"Come on, Annie! It's time to go home!" yelled Jack.

But Annie didn't answer.

Jack waited.

"Annie!" he called again.

"Jack! Jack!" Annie shouted. "Come here! Quick!"

Jack groaned. "This better be good," he said.

Jack left the road and headed into the woods. The trees were lit with a golden late-afternoon light.

"Over here!" called Annie.

Annie was standing under a tall oak tree. "Look!" she said. She pointed at a rope ladder. It was hanging down from high in the tree.

"Wow," Jack whispered.

At the top of the tree was a tree house, tucked between two branches.

"That must be the highest tree house in the world," said Annie.

"Who built it?" asked Jack. "I've never seen it before."

"I don't know. But I'm going up," said Annie.

"No! We don't know who it belongs to," said Jack.

"Just for a teeny minute," said Annie. She started up the ladder.

"Annie, come back!" said Jack.

But Annie kept climbing. She climbed all the way up to the tallest branches.

Jack sighed. "Annie, it's almost dark! We have to go home!"

Annie disappeared inside the tree house.

"Annie!" Jack called.

Jack waited a moment. He was about to call again when Annie poked her head out of the tree house window.

"Books!" Annie shouted.

"What?" Jack said.

"It's filled with books!" said Annie.

Oh, man! Jack thought. He loved books.

Jack pushed his glasses into place. He gripped the sides of the rope ladder and started up.

CHAPTER TWO

THE MONSTER

Jack crawled into the tree house.

"Wow," he said. The tree house *was* filled with books. Books were everywhere—very old books with dusty covers and new books with shiny, bright covers.

"Look," said Annie. "You can see far away." She was peering out the tree house window.

Jack looked out the window with her. Below were the tops of the other trees. In the distance he could see the Frog Creek library and the elementary school and the park.

Annie pointed in the other direction.

"There's our house," she said.

Annie was right. Jack could see their white wooden house with its green porch. In the yard next door was their neighbor's black dog, Henry. He looked very tiny.

"Hi, Henry!" shouted Annie.

"Shush! We're not supposed to be up here," said Jack.

Jack glanced around the tree house again. He noticed that bookmarks were sticking out of many of the books. "I wonder who owns all these books," he said.

"I like this one," said Annie. She picked up a

book with a castle on the cover.

"Here's a book about Pennsylvania," said Jack. He turned to the page with the bookmark.

"Hey, here's a picture of Frog Creek," said Jack. "It's a picture of *these* woods!"

"Oh, here's a book for you," said Annie. She held up a book about dinosaurs. A blue silk bookmark was sticking out of it.

"Let me see," said Jack. He set his backpack down on the floor and grabbed the book from Annie.

"Okay. You look at that one, and I'll look at the one about castles," said Annie.

"No, we'd better not," said Jack. "We don't know who these books belong to."

But even as he said this, Jack was opening the

dinosaur book to the place where the bookmark was. He couldn't help himself.

Jack turned to a picture of an ancient flying reptile. He recognized it as a Pteranodon. He touched the huge bat-like wings in the picture.

"Wow," whispered Jack. "I wish we could go to the time of Pteranodons."

Jack studied the picture of the odd-looking creature soaring through the sky.

"Ahhh!" screamed Annie.

"What?" said Jack.

"A monster!" Annie cried. She pointed out the tree house window.

"Stop pretending, Annie," said Jack.

"No, really!" said Annie.

Jack looked out the window.

A giant creature was gliding above the tree-tops! It had a long, weird crest on the back of its head, a skinny beak, and huge bat-like wings!

It was a real live Pteranodon!

The creature swooped through the sky. It looked like a glider plane! It was coming straight toward the tree house!

"Get down!" cried Annie.

Jack and Annie crouched on the floor.

The wind started to blow.

The tree house started to spin.

It spun faster and faster.

Then everything was still.

Absolutely still.

CHAPTER THREE

WHERE IS HERE?

Jack opened his eyes. Sunlight slanted through the window.

The tree house was still high up in a tree.

But it wasn't the *same* tree.

"Where are we?" said Annie. She and Jack looked out the window.

The Pteranodon was soaring through the sky. The ground was covered with ferns and tall grass. There was a winding stream, a sloping hill, and volcanoes in the distance.

"I—I don't know where we are," said Jack.

The Pteranodon glided down to the base of the tree. It landed on the ground and stood very still.

"So what just happened to us?" said Annie.

"Well . . . ," said Jack. "I was looking at the picture in the book—"

"And you said, 'Wow, I wish we could go to the time of Pteranodons,' " said Annie.

"Yeah. And then we saw a Pteranodon in the Frog Creek woods," said Jack.

"Yeah. And then the wind got loud. And the

tree house started spinning," said Annie.

"And we landed here," said Jack.

"And we landed here," said Annie.

"So that means . . . ," said Jack.

"So that means . . . what?" said Annie.

"I don't know," said Jack. He shook his head. "None of this can be real."

Annie looked out the window again. "But *he*'s real," she said. "He's *very* real."

Jack looked out the window with her again. The

Pteranodon was standing at the base of the tree like a guard. His giant wings were spread out on either side of him.

"Hi!" Annie shouted.

"Shhh!" said Jack. "We're not supposed to be here."

"But where is *here*?" said Annie.

"I don't know," said Jack.

"Hi! Who are you?" Annie called to the Pteranodon.

The creature just looked up at her.

"Are you nuts? He can't talk," said Jack. "But maybe the book can tell us."

Jack looked down at the book. He read the words under the picture:

This flying reptile lived in the Cretaceous Period. It vanished 65 million years ago with the dinosaurs.

"That's impossible!" said Jack. "We can't have gone to a time sixty-five million years ago!"

"Jack," said Annie. "He's nice."

"Nice?" said Jack.

"Yeah, I can tell," said Annie. "Let's go down to him."

"Go down?" said Jack.

Annie started down the rope ladder.

"Hey, come back," said Jack.

But Annie kept going.

"Annie, wait!" Jack called.

Annie dropped to the ground. She stepped boldly up to the ancient creature.

CHAPTER FOUR

HENRY

Jack gasped as Annie reached out her hand toward the Pteranodon.

Oh, no, he thought. Annie was always trying to make friends with animals, but this was going too far.

"Don't get too close to him, Annie!" Jack shouted.

Annie touched the Pteranodon's crest. She stroked his neck. She was talking to him.

What in the world is she saying? Jack wondered.

He took a deep breath. Okay. He would go down, too. It would be good to examine a Pteranodon. He could take notes like a scientist.

Jack started down the rope ladder. When he reached the ground, he was only a few feet away from the creature.

The Pteranodon stared at Jack. His eyes were bright and alert.

"He's soft, Jack," said Annie. "He feels like Henry."

Jack snorted. "He's no dog, Annie."

"Feel him, Jack," said Annie.

Jack didn't move.

"Don't think, Jack. Just do it," Annie said.

Jack stepped forward. He reached out very cautiously. He brushed his hand down the creature's neck.

Interesting, Jack thought. A thin layer of fuzz covered the Pteranodon's skin.

"Soft, huh?" said Annie.

Jack reached into his backpack and pulled out a pencil and a notebook. He wrote:

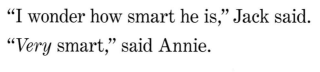

fuzzy skin

"What are you doing?" asked Annie.

"Taking notes," said Jack. "We're probably the first people in the whole world to ever see a real live Pteranodon."

Jack looked at the Pteranodon again. The bony crest on top of his head was longer than Jack's arm.

"I wonder how smart he is," Jack said.

"*Very* smart," said Annie.

"Don't count on it," said Jack. "His brain's probably no bigger than a bean."

"No, he's very smart. I can feel it," said Annie. "I'm going to call him Henry."

Jack wrote in his notebook:

small brain?

Jack looked at the creature again. "Maybe he's a mutant," he said.

The Pteranodon tilted his head.

Annie laughed. "He's not a mutant, Jack."

"Well, what's he doing here, then? Where is this place?" said Jack.

Annie leaned close to the Pteranodon. "Do you know where we are, Henry?" she asked softly.

The creature fixed his eyes on Annie. His long jaws were opening and closing like a giant pair of scissors.

"Are you trying to talk to me, Henry?" asked Annie.

"Forget it, Annie." Jack wrote in his notebook:

mouth like scissors

"Did we come to a time long ago, Henry?" asked Annie. "Is this a place from long ago?"

Suddenly Annie gasped. "Jack!"

Jack looked up.

Annie was pointing toward the hill. On top stood a huge dinosaur!

CHAPTER FIVE

GOLD IN THE GRASS

"Go! *Go!*" said Jack. He threw his notebook into his pack. He pushed Annie toward the rope ladder.

"Bye, Henry!" she said.

"Go!" said Jack. He gave Annie another push.

"Quit it!" she said. But she started up the ladder. Jack scrambled after her.

Jack and Annie tumbled into the tree house. They were panting as they looked out the window at the dinosaur. It was standing on the hilltop, eating flowers off a tree.

"Oh, man," whispered Jack. "We *are* in a time long ago!"

The dinosaur looked like a huge rhinoceros with three horns instead of one. It had two long horns above its eyes, and another one grew out from its nose. It had a big shield-like thing behind its head.

"Triceratops!" said Jack.

"Does he eat people?" whispered Annie.

"I'll look it up." Jack grabbed the dinosaur book. He flipped through the pages.

"There!" said Jack, pointing to a picture of a Triceratops. He read the caption:

The Triceratops lived in the late Cretaceous Period. This plant-eating dinosaur weighed over 12,000 pounds.

Jack slammed the book shut. "Just plants. No meat."

"Good!" said Annie. "Let's go see him up close."

"Are you crazy?" said Jack.

"Don't you want to take notes about him?" asked Annie. "We're probably the first people in the whole world to ever see a real live Triceratops."

Jack sighed. Annie was right.

"Okay, let's go," he said.

Jack shoved the dinosaur book into his pack.

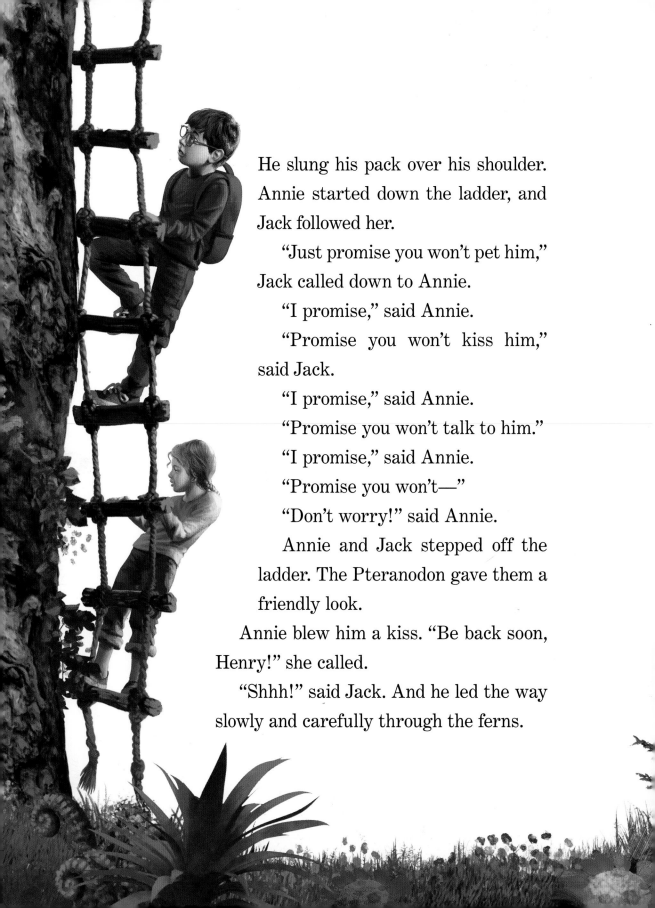

He slung his pack over his shoulder. Annie started down the ladder, and Jack followed her.

"Just promise you won't pet him," Jack called down to Annie.

"I promise," said Annie.

"Promise you won't kiss him," said Jack.

"I promise," said Annie.

"Promise you won't talk to him."

"I promise," said Annie.

"Promise you won't—"

"Don't worry!" said Annie.

Annie and Jack stepped off the ladder. The Pteranodon gave them a friendly look.

Annie blew him a kiss. "Be back soon, Henry!" she called.

"Shhh!" said Jack. And he led the way slowly and carefully through the ferns.

When Jack and Annie reached the bottom of the hill, they knelt behind a bush. Annie started to speak, but Jack quickly put his finger to his lips. Then he and Annie peeked out at the Triceratops.

The dinosaur was bigger than a truck. He was eating the flowers off a magnolia tree.

Jack slipped his notebook out of his pack. He wrote:

eats flowers

Annie nudged him.

Jack ignored her. He studied the Triceratops again. He wrote:

eats slowly

Annie nudged him harder.
Jack looked at her.

Annie pointed to herself. She walked her fingers through the air. She pointed to the dinosaur. She smiled.

Is she teasing? Jack wondered.

Annie waved at Jack.

Jack started to grab her.

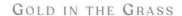

She laughed and jumped away. She fell into the grass in full view of the Triceratops!

"Get back!" whispered Jack.

Too late. The big dinosaur had spotted Annie. He gazed down at her from the hilltop. Half of a magnolia flower was sticking out of his mouth.

"Oops," said Annie.

"Get back!" Jack said again.

"He looks nice, Jack," Annie said.

"Nice? Watch out for his horns, Annie!" said Jack.

The Triceratops gazed calmly down at Annie. Then he turned and loped down the side of the hill.

"Bye!" said Annie. She turned back to Jack. "See?"

Jack grunted. But he wrote in his notebook:

nice

"Come on. Let's look around some more," said Annie.

As Jack started after Annie, he saw something glittering in the tall grass.

Jack reached down and picked it up. It was a gold medallion.

A letter was engraved on the medallion: a fancy *M*.

"Oh, man. Someone was here before us!" Jack said softly.

CHAPTER SIX

DINOSAUR VALLEY

"Annie, look at this!" Jack called. "Look what I found!"

Annie had gone up to the hilltop. She was picking a flower from the magnolia tree.

"Annie, look! A medallion!" shouted Jack.

But Annie wasn't paying attention to Jack. She was staring at something on the other side of the hill.

"Oh, wow!" she said. Clutching her magnolia flower, she took off down the hill.

"Annie, come back!" Jack shouted.

But Annie had disappeared.

"Oh, brother," Jack muttered. He stuffed the gold medallion into his jeans pocket.

Then Jack heard Annie shriek.

"Annie?" he said.

Jack heard another sound as well—a deep, bellowing sound, like a tuba.

"Jack! Come here, quick!" Annie called.

Jack raced up the hill. When he got to the top, he gasped.

The valley below was filled with nests—big nests made out of mud. The nests were filled with tiny dinosaurs!

Annie was crouching next to one of the nests. Towering over her was a gigantic duck-billed dinosaur!

"Don't panic. Don't move," said Jack. He stepped slowly down the hill toward Annie.

The huge dinosaur was waving her arms and making her tuba sound.

Jack stopped. He didn't want to get too close.

He knelt on the ground. "Okay. Move toward me. Slowly," he said.

Annie started to stand up.

"Don't stand! Crawl," said Jack.

Clutching her flower, Annie crawled toward Jack.

Still bellowing, the duck-billed dinosaur followed her.

Annie froze.

"Keep going," Jack said.

Annie started crawling again.

Jack inched farther down the hill, until he was just an arm's distance from Annie. He reached out and grabbed her hand. He pulled Annie toward him.

"Stay down," Jack said. He crouched next to her. "Bow your head. Pretend to chew."

"Chew?" said Annie.

"Yes," said Jack. "I read that's what you do if a mean dog comes at you."

"She's no dog, Jack," said Annie.

"Just chew," said Jack.

Jack and Annie both bowed their heads and pretended to chew. Soon the dinosaur grew quiet.

Jack looked up. "I don't think she's mad anymore," he said.

"You saved me," said Annie. "Thanks."

"You have to use your brain, Annie," said Jack.

"You can't just go running to a nest of babies. There's always a mother nearby."

Annie stood up.

"Annie, don't!" said Jack.

Too late.

Annie held out her magnolia flower to the dinosaur.

"I'm sorry I made you worry about your babies," she said.

The dinosaur moved closer to Annie. She grabbed the flower from her hand. She reached for another.

"No more," said Annie.

The dinosaur let out a sad tuba sound.

"But there are more flowers up there," Annie said. She pointed to the top of the hill. "I'll get you some."

Annie hurried up the hill.

The dinosaur waddled after her.

Jack quickly looked at the dinosaur babies. Some were crawling out of their nests.

Where are the other mothers? Jack wondered.

Jack took out the dinosaur book. He flipped through the pages. He found a picture of some duck-billed dinosaurs. He read the caption:

**The Anatosauruses lived in colonies.
While a few mothers babysat the nests,
others looked for food.**

So there were probably more mothers close by,
looking for food.

"Hey, Jack!" Annie called.

Jack looked up. Annie was at the top of the
hill, feeding magnolia flowers to the giant
Anatosaurus!

"Guess what?" Annie said. "She's nice, too."

Suddenly the Anatosaurus made her terrible
tuba sound. Annie crouched down and started to
chew.

The dinosaur charged down the hill. She seemed
afraid of something.

Jack put the book on top of his pack. He hurried
to Annie.

"I wonder why she ran away," said Annie. "We
were starting to be friends."

Jack looked around. What he saw in the distance almost made him faint!

An enormous monster was coming across the plain.

The monster was walking on two strong legs. It was swinging a long, thick tail and dangling two tiny arms.

It had a huge head—and its jaws were wide open.

Even from far away Jack could see its long, gleaming teeth.

"Tyrannosaurus rex!" whispered Jack.

READY, SET, GO!

"Run, Annie! Run!" cried Jack. "Run to the tree house!"

Jack and Annie dashed down the hill together. They ran through the tall grass and ferns and past the Pteranodon.

They scrambled up the rope ladder and tumbled into the tree house.

Annie leaped to the window.

"It's going away!" she said, panting.

Jack pushed his glasses into place. He looked out the window with Annie.

The Tyrannosaurus was wandering off.

But then the monster stopped and turned around.

"Duck!" said Jack.

The two of them ducked their heads.

After a long moment, they peeked out the window again.

"Coast clear," said Jack.

"Yay," whispered Annie.

"We have to get out of here," said Jack.

"You made a wish before," said Annie.

"Right," said Jack. He took a deep breath. "I wish we could go back to Frog Creek!"

Nothing happened.

"I said I wish—" started Jack.

"Wait," said Annie. "You were looking at a picture in the dinosaur book. Remember?"

"Oh, no, I left the book and my pack on the hill!" said Jack. "I have to go back!"

"Forget it," said Annie.

"I can't," said Jack. "The

book doesn't belong to us. Plus my notebook with all my notes is in my pack. And my—"

"Okay, okay!" said Annie.

"I'll hurry!" said Jack. He climbed quickly down the ladder and leaped to the ground.

Jack raced past the Pteranodon, through the ferns, through the tall grass, and up the hill.

He looked down.

His pack was lying on the ground. On top of it was the dinosaur book.

But now the valley below was filled with Anatosauruses. They were all standing guard around the nests.

Where had they been? Did fear of the Tyrannosaurus send them home?

Jack took a deep breath. *Ready! Set! Go!* he thought.

He charged down the hill. He ran to his backpack. He scooped it up. He grabbed the dinosaur book.

Jack heard a terrible tuba sound! Then another, and another! All the Anatosauruses were bellowing at him!

Jack took off.

He raced up to the hilltop.

He started down the hill.

He stopped.

The Tyrannosaurus rex was back! It was standing between Jack and the tree house!

CHAPTER EIGHT

A GIANT SHADOW

Jack jumped behind the magnolia tree.

His heart was beating so fast he could hardly think.

He peeked out at the giant monster. The horrible-looking creature was opening and closing its huge jaws. Its teeth were as big as steak knives.

Don't panic, thought Jack. *Think.*

He peered down at the valley.

Good. The duck-billed dinosaurs were sticking close to their nests.

Jack looked back at the Tyrannosaurus.

Good. The monster still didn't seem to know he was there.

Don't panic. Think. Think. Maybe there's information in the book.

Jack opened the dinosaur book. He found Tyrannosaurus rex. He read:

Tyrannosaurus rex was one of the largest meat-eating land animals of all time. If it were alive today, it could eat a human in one bite.

Great, thought Jack. The book was no help at all.

Jack tried to think clearly. He couldn't hide on the other side of the hill. The Anatosauruses might stampede.

He couldn't run to the tree house. The Tyrannosaurus might run faster.

Maybe he should just wait for the monster to leave.

Jack peeked around the tree.

The Tyrannosaurus had wandered *closer* to the hill.

Something caught Jack's eye. Annie was coming down the rope ladder!

A Giant Shadow

Is she nuts? What is she doing? Jack wondered.
Jack watched Annie hop off the ladder.

Annie hurried over to the Pteranodon. She was talking to him. She was flapping her arms. She pointed at Jack, at the sky, at the tree house.

She is *nuts!* Jack thought.

"Go! Go back up in the tree!" Jack whispered. "Go!"

Jack heard a roar.

The Tyrannosaurus rex was looking in his direction.

Jack hit the ground.

The Tyrannosaurus rex was coming toward the hill.

Jack felt the ground shaking.

What should I do? Jack wondered. *Should I run? Crawl back into Dinosaur Valley? Climb the magnolia tree?*

Suddenly a giant shadow covered Jack. He looked up.

The Pteranodon was gliding overhead. The giant creature sailed toward the top of the hill.

He was heading toward Jack.

CHAPTER NINE

THE AMAZING RIDE

The Pteranodon coasted down to the ground.

He stared at Jack with his bright, alert eyes.

What was Jack supposed to do? Climb on? *But I'm too heavy*, thought Jack.

Jack looked at the Tyrannosaurus. It was starting up the hill. Its giant teeth were flashing in the sunlight.

Okay, thought Jack. *Don't think! Just do it!*

Jack put his book in his pack. Then he climbed onto the Pteranodon's back. He held on tightly.

The creature moved forward. He spread his wings—and lifted off the ground!

Jack nearly fell off as they teetered this way and that.

The Pteranodon steadied himself and rose into the sky.

Jack looked down. The Tyrannosaurus was staring up at him and chomping the air.

The Pteranodon glided away.

He sailed over the hilltop and over the valley.

He circled above all the duck-billed dinosaurs and all the nests filled with babies.

Then the Pteranodon soared out over the plain— over the Triceratops, who was grazing in the high grass.

Jack felt like a bird. The wind was rushing through his hair. The air smelled sweet and fresh.

Jack whooped and laughed. He couldn't believe it! He was riding on the back of an ancient flying reptile!

The Pteranodon sailed over the stream and over the ferns and bushes. Then he carried Jack down to the base of the oak tree.

When they came to a stop, Jack slid off the creature's back and landed on the ground.

The Pteranodon took off again and glided into the sky.

"Bye, Henry!" called Jack.

"Jack! Are you okay?" Annie shouted from the tree house.

Jack pushed his glasses into place. He kept staring at the Pteranodon.

"Jack!" Annie called.

Jack looked up at Annie. He smiled.

"Thanks for saving my life," he said. "That was really fun."

"Thank Henry, not me!" said Annie. "Come on! Climb up!"

Jack tried to stand. His legs were wobbly. He felt a bit dizzy.

"Hurry!" shouted Annie. "It's coming!"

Jack looked around. The Tyrannosaurus was heading straight toward him! Jack bolted to the ladder. He started climbing.

"Hurry! Hurry!" screamed Annie.

Jack reached the top and scrambled into the tree house.

"It's coming toward the tree!" Annie cried.

The dinosaur slammed against the oak tree. The tree house shook like a leaf in the wind.

Jack and Annie tumbled into the books.

"Make a wish to go home!" cried Annie.

"We need the book! The Pennsylvania book!" said Jack. "Where is it?"

They both searched madly around the tree house.

"Found it!" said Jack.

He grabbed the book and flipped through the pages. He found the photograph of the Frog Creek woods.

Jack pointed to the picture in the book.

"I wish we could go home!" he shouted.

The wind began to blow.

Jack closed his eyes. He held on tightly to Annie.

The tree house started to spin.

It spun faster and faster.

Then everything was still.

Absolutely still.

CHAPTER TEN

HOME BEFORE DARK

J ack heard a bird singing.

He opened his eyes. He was still pointing at the picture of the Frog Creek woods.

He peeked out the tree house window. Outside he saw the exact same view as the picture in the book.

"We're home," whispered Annie.

The woods were lit with a golden late-afternoon light. The sun was about to set.

No time had passed since they'd left Frog Creek.

"Ja-ack! An-nie!" a voice called from the distance.

"That's Mom," said Annie.

Jack saw their mother far away. She was standing in front of their house. She looked tiny.

"An-nie! Ja-ack!" she called.

Annie stuck her head out the window and shouted, "Coming!"

Jack still felt dazed. He just stared at Annie.

"What happened to us?" he said.

"We took a trip in a magic tree house," said Annie simply.

"But it's the same time as when we left," said Jack.

Annie shrugged.

"How did it take us so far away?" said Jack. "And so long ago?"

"You looked at a picture in a book and said you wished we could go there," said Annie. "And the magic tree house took us there."

"But *how*?" said Jack. "And who built this magic tree house? Who put all these books here?"

"A magic person, I guess," said Annie.

"Oh, look," said Jack. "I almost forgot about this."

Jack reached into his pocket and pulled out the

gold medallion. "Someone lost this back there," he said, "in dinosaur land. Look, there's a letter *M* on it."

Annie's eyes got round. "You think *M* stands for *magic person*?" she asked.

"I don't know," said Jack. "I just know someone went to that place before us."

"Ja-ack! An-nie!" their mom called again.

"Coming!" Annie shouted again.

Jack put the gold medallion back in his pocket. He pulled the dinosaur book out of his pack and put it back with all the other books.

Then he and Annie took one last look around the tree house.

"Good-bye, house," whispered Annie.

Jack slung his backpack over his shoulders. Annie started down the rope ladder. Jack followed.

Seconds later they hopped onto the ground and started walking out of the woods.

"No one's going to believe our story," said Jack.

"So let's not tell anyone," said Annie.

"Dad won't believe it," said Jack.

"He'll say it was a dream," said Annie.

"Mom won't believe it," said Jack.

"She'll say it was pretend."

"My teacher won't believe it," said Jack.

"She'll say you're nuts," said Annie.

"We'd better not tell anyone," said Jack.

"I already said that," said Annie.

Jack sighed. "I think I'm starting not to believe it myself," he said.

They left the woods and started up the road toward their house.

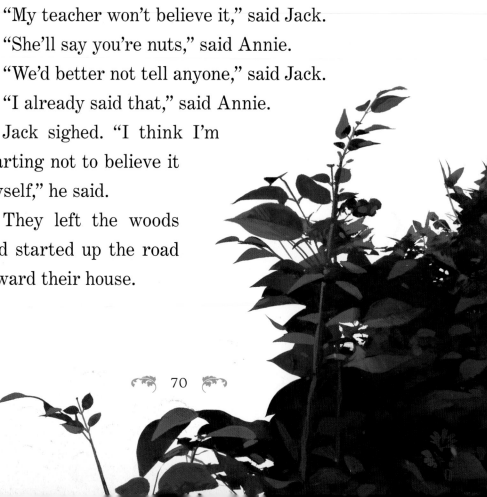

As they walked past all the houses on their street, the trip to dinosaur time *did* seem more and more like a dream.

Only *this* world and *this* time seemed real.

Jack reached into his pocket. He clasped the gold medallion.

He felt the engraving of the letter *M*. It made his fingers tingle.

Jack laughed. Suddenly he felt very happy.

He couldn't explain what had happened today. But he knew for sure that their trip in the magic tree house had been real.

Absolutely real.

"Tomorrow," Jack said softly, "we'll goww back to the woods."

"Of course," said Annie.

"And we'll climb up to the tree house," said Jack.

"Of course," said Annie.

"And we'll see what happens next," said Jack.

"Of course," said Annie. "Race you!"
And they took off together, running for home.

A Note from the Author

When *Dinosaurs Before Dark* was first published in 1992, I had no idea that twenty-eight years later, I would still be writing books for the Magic Tree House series and having more fun than ever. I owe much gratitude to the millions of young readers (and their parents!) who have traveled in the tree house with Jack and Annie, and to the countless educators who have used the series to teach reading, social studies, history, geography, and science.

It's been a joy to meet teachers all over the world who have shared their Magic Tree House classroom projects with me, including dioramas, homemade tree houses, and the drawings and creative writing of their students. As a gift to all the teachers who have embraced the Magic Tree House, I created the Magic Tree House Classroom Adventures Program at MTHClassroomAdventures.org. In addition, Magic Tree House fans can experience adventure and learning through the educational games on MagicTreeHouse.com.

The series has also given me the opportunity to work more closely with my family and friends. My sister, Natalie Pope Boyce, has written more than thirty-five Magic Tree House Fact Trackers, non-fiction companions to my books. My husband, Will Osborne, along with writing the first eight Fact Trackers, created a Magic Tree House planetarium show as well as a number of Magic Tree House musicals with our good friends, composer Randy Courts and playwright Jenny Laird. And now Jenny is helping to adapt the series for new graphic novel editions that will start coming out in 2021!

Over the years, our community of writers, artists, editors, educators, and families has spread all over the world. Jack and Annie's adventures have been translated into thirty-five languages. Will and I have traveled to Japan, Germany, Italy, and France to meet young readers and discovered that children everywhere have one thing in common: they love to travel in their imaginations with Jack and Annie to different times and places, and learn about the world.

For all those who feel connected to the series, Random House is presenting this new edition of *Dinosaurs Before Dark*, re-illustrated for the first time. Whether it's a young person discovering the magic of reading, a teacher reading to a class, or a family reading together before bedtime, I hope this full-color edition will take young (and old) readers across time and space into the astonishing pre-historic world of dinosaurs.

Mary Pope Osborne

Uncover more
dinosaur facts with the
Magic Tree House Fact Tracker
Dinosaurs

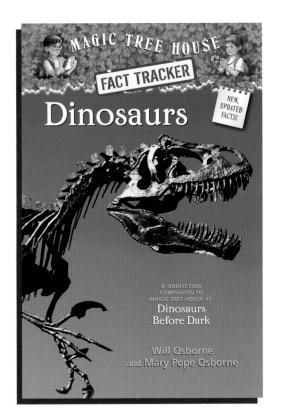

Turn the page for a sneak peek. . . .

Tyrannosaurus rex

(ty-RAN-uh-SOAR-us RECKS)

This name means "tyrant-lizard king."

T. rex is the most famous flesh-eating dinosaur of all time. It had sharp teeth—many were more than six inches long. It had a head the size of a bathtub. One *T. rex* mouthful of food could feed a whole family of humans for weeks.

   T. rex had big, strong legs. But its arms were so short they couldn't even reach its mouth. Paleontologists are still trying to find out how—or even *if*—*T. rex* used its tiny arms.

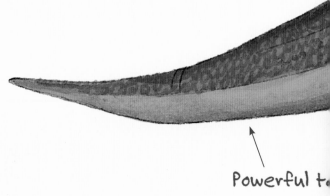

Powerful t

BIG head

Almost 20 feet tall

BIG mouth

BIG teeth

Tiny arms

Strong legs

Triceratops
(try-SEHR-uh-tops)

Triceratops had a face like a scary Halloween mask. It had a beak like a parrot's. It had three long horns.

Paleontologists say that *Triceratops* used their horns mostly to fight off other dinosaurs that were trying to eat them. But they also think that sometimes two male *Triceratops* would lock horns and fight with each other over a female.

BOO!

Three horns

Neck shield
(called a <u>frill</u>)

Beak like
a parrot's

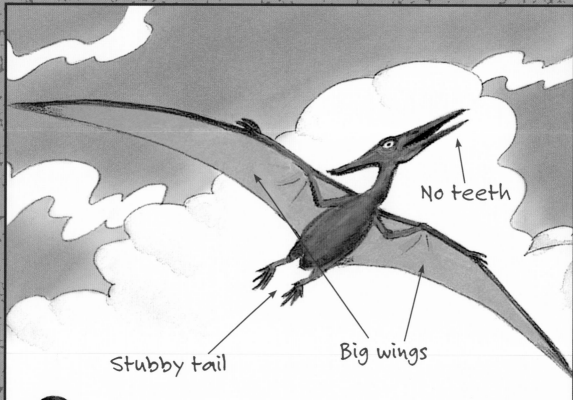

No teeth

Stubby tail

Big wings

Pteranodon
(teh-RAN-uh-don)

Pteranodon had a long beak and a long, bony crest on the back of its head. It probably needed the crest to help balance its beak when it was swooping down to catch fish.

LET THE MAGIC TREE HOUSE WHISK

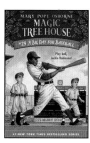

HAVE YOU READ ALL THE ADVENTURES?